The
Tiara
Club
✦ AT RUBY MANSIONS ✦

The Tiara Club

Princess Charlotte *and the* Birthday Ball
Princess Katie *and the* Silver Pony
Princess Daisy *and the* Dazzling Dragon
Princess Alice *and the* Magical Mirror
Princess Sophia *and the* Sparkling Surprise
Princess Emily *and the* Substitute Fairy

The Tiara Club at Silver Towers

Princess Charlotte *and the* Enchanted Rose
Princess Katie *and the* Mixed-up Potion
Princess Daisy *and the* Magical Merry-Go-Round
Princess Alice *and the* Glass Slipper
Princess Sophia *and the* Prince's Party
Princess Emily *and the* Wishing Star

The Tiara Club at Ruby Mansions

Princess Chloe *and the* Primrose Petticoats
Princess Jessica *and the* Best-Friend Bracelet
Princess Georgia *and the* Shimmering Pearl
Princess Olivia *and the* Velvet Cape
Princess Lauren *and the* Diamond Necklace

VIVIAN FRENCH

The Tiara Club

✦ AT RUBY MANSIONS ✦

Princess Amy
AND THE
Forgetting Dust

KATHERINE TEGEN BOOKS
HarperTrophy®
An Imprint of HarperCollins Publishers

The Tiara Club at Ruby Mansions:
Princess Amy and the Forgetting Dust
Text copyright © 2008 by Vivian French
Illustrations copyright © 2008 by Orchard Books
All rights reserved. Printed in the United States of America.
A paperback edition of this book was published in the United
Kingdom in 2007 by Orchard Books.

www.harpercollinschildrens.com

Library of Congress Catalog Card Number: 2007905254
ISBN 978-0-06-143489-1
❖
First U.S. edition, 2008

For Princess Sophie,
and Princess Isabelle too xxx
—V. F.

The Royal Palace Academy
for the Preparation of Perfect Princesses
(Known to our students as "The Princess Academy")

OUR SCHOOL MOTTO:
*A Perfect Princess always thinks of others before herself,
and is kind, caring, and truthful.*

**Ruby Mansions offers a complete education for
Tiara Club princesses with emphasis on the
creative arts. The curriculum includes:**

Innovative Ideas for our Friendship Festival

Designing Floral Bouquets (all thorns will be removed)

Ballet for Grace and Poise

*A visit to the Diamond Exhibition
(on the joyous occasion of Queen Fabiola's birthday)*

**Our principal, Queen Fabiola, is present at all times,
and students are in the excellent care of the head fairy
godmother, Fairy G., and her assistant, Fairy Angora.**

OUR RESIDENT STAFF & VISITING EXPERTS INCLUDE:

KING BERNARDO IV *(Ruby Mansions Governor)*

LADY ARAMINTA *(Princess Academy Matron)*

LADY HARRIS *(Secretary to Queen Fabiola)*

QUEEN MOTHER MATILDA *(Etiquette, Posture, and Flower Arranging)*

We award tiara points to encourage our
Tiara Club princesses toward the next level.
All princesses who earn enough points at Ruby
Mansions will attend a celebration ball, where they
will be presented with their Ruby Sashes.

Ruby Sash Tiara Club princesses are invited
to go on to Pearl Palace, our very special
residence for Perfect Princesses, where they may
continue their education at a higher level.

PLEASE NOTE:
Princesses are expected to arrive
at the Academy with a *minimum* of:

TWENTY BALL GOWNS
*(with all necessary hoops,
petticoats, etc.)*

TWELVE DAY-DRESSES

SEVEN GOWNS
*suitable for garden parties
and other special daytime
occasions*

TWELVE TIARAS

DANCING SHOES
five pairs

VELVET SLIPPERS
three pairs

RIDING BOOTS
two pairs

*Cloaks, muffs, stoles, gloves,
and other essential
accessories, as required*

Hello to all princesses—especially you! I'm Princess Amy from the Poppy Room. Don't you just love being here at Ruby Mansions? Although I'm sure Pearl Palace will be so much fun—as long as you're there, and all my other friends from the Poppy Room too. I couldn't stand it without Chloe, Jessica, Georgia, Olivia, and Lauren. I wonder if the horrible twins, Diamonde and Gruella, will be at Pearl Palace? Ooooh! They're so mean! Especially Diamonde . . .

Chapter One

"One, two, three, *twirl*! One, two, three, *twirl*!"

Fairy Angora waved her wand in time to the music. We did our best to follow her instructions, but it wasn't easy. I kept getting dizzy and bumping into my friends.

"Please, Fairy Angora, couldn't you help us with a bit of magic?" As I spoke, I found I'd twirled myself into a corner and had to come out backward. "I'm not very good at ballet!"

Fairy Angora laughed. (She's the assistant fairy godmother at the Princess Academy.) "That would be

cheating, my angel," she said.
"Ballet teaches you grace and poise.
If I did it by magic, it would fade
away, and then what would happen
at tomorrow's end-of-term dance
concert?"

Princess Diamonde sniggered.
"Amy will be stomping around like
a big fat elephant!"

Fairy Angora gave her a frosty look. "That, Diamonde, is not a kind or helpful thing to say. Please show us your very best pirouette."

Diamonde looked terribly pleased with herself as she stepped forward.

"Certainly, Fairy Angora," she said. Then she did three perfect pirouettes one after the other and ended with the most beautiful curtsey. We couldn't help bursting into a big round of applause—she was really good. Of course Diamonde looked more smug than ever.

"Well done, Diamonde," Fairy

Angora said, but she didn't sound as pleased as she usually does when one of us does something right. "I can see you've had lots of lessons. You have earned two tiara points." And then she went to talk to the musicians.

"Diamonde and I have been going to ballet since we were three," Princess Gruella told us. "Mommy says it's very important that princesses like us have every opportunity to learn to be graceful."

"That's right!" Diamonde gave

me a snooty look. "I doubt *your* parents thought these things mattered, and that's why you're so hopeless."

I stared at her in amazement. "You don't know anything about my parents!" I said. "How can you say such things? If you really want to know, I did take ballet when I was little, but . . ." I hesitated. Did I really want Diamonde and Gruella to know about my family? But then I thought, *Hey! I'm proud of my mom and dad!* So I went on. "But the lessons were too expensive. They don't have much money, but they always want me to have the best. Why, they even canceled a wonderful Royal Tour so I could come here in their very special traveling coach."

Diamonde stuck her nose in the air. "Huh! I saw you arrive. That wasn't a very special coach. Why, it wasn't even gold. Don't you know that Perfect Princesses always travel in golden coaches?"

Luckily for me, Fairy Angora came hurrying back just then, otherwise I would have said something that would not have been at all princessy.

"Did I hear you mention a golden coach?" she asked, and she looked very anxious. "Oh, no! Has somebody told you Queen Fabiola's secret?"

Of course we all shook our heads, except for Diamonde. She winked at Gruella and said, "Well, someone might have told us about

a very special coach. . . ."

It was obvious she didn't really know anything, but Fairy Angora didn't seem to notice. She sat down on a chair looking very upset. "Queen Fabiola will be very angry! She wanted it to be a wonderful surprise—the most beautiful golden coach you've ever seen to take you to the End-of-Term Celebration Ball!"

Chapter Two

We didn't know what to say. Fairy Angora had just told us our principal's secret, and we weren't supposed to know!

Gruella raised her hand. "How will we all fit into one coach?" she asked. "And why isn't the ball going to be here—*ouch*!" She turned and glared at Diamonde. "Why did you pinch me?"

"Sshhhh!" Diamonde hissed, but she was too late. Fairy Angora was staring at her, her eyes wide.

"You didn't know about the queen's secret surprise, did you, Diamonde? Because if someone really had told you, you'd know the ball was going to be at Pearl Palace. And you'd know that only the very best dancers will be traveling in the golden coach. You were just pretending you knew!"

Diamonde shuffled her feet. "I only said someone might have told us," she muttered.

Fairy Angora clutched her wand. "Oh, how silly I am." She looked around at all of us and her cheeks were very pink. "Please, my angels, please try to forget what I said. We want our princesses to always try their best, not just because they want to win a place in a wonderful coach."

"It's all right, Fairy Angora," Princess Olivia said. "We won't even think about the coach."

And we all nodded—except for Diamonde.

She gave Fairy Angora a sly look. "If we pretend we don't know about this coach," she said, "will we get extra tiara points for ballet?"

"That's right!" Gruella agreed.

"Lots of tiara points so we're sure to ride in the coach!"

I was shocked. We all know that Perfect Princesses never ever talk like that.

Fairy Angora turned pale, then she folded her arms and frowned.

"Princess Diamonde and Princess Gruella," she said, "just this once I will overlook the way you have spoken to me, because I should never have asked you to keep a secret." She stopped and looked at me. "Princess Amy, would you be an angel and run along to Fairy G.'s office? Please ask her if I can borrow her Forgetting Dust." She turned back to the class. "I'll sprinkle a little in this room and all of you will forget what I have said. That way none of us will need to worry about tiara points and the golden coach. And now, let's go back to our ballet lesson."

As I hurried out the door, I saw Diamonde and Gruella looking very disappointed.

Fairy G. is the head fairy god-mother, and she has offices all over the Princess Academy. Her room in Ruby Mansions was at the end of a long marble hallway. The maids were busy polishing the floor as I walked up to her door and knocked.

"Come in," she called, and I went inside.

Fairy G. was sitting behind her desk knitting something ruby red and sparkly. She saw me looking and smiled. "It's a shawl to wear to the End-of-Term Celebration Ball," she explained. "For when you're presented with your Ruby Sashes. What can I do for you, Amy dear?"

I curtsied and told her that Fairy Angora needed to borrow some Forgetting Dust. Fairy G. raised her eyebrows, but all she said was, "Of course. You'll find it over there on the shelf. It's the yellow bottle."

Fairy G.'s shelves were stuffed

with jars and bags and bottles. I think she must have used magic to find what she wanted, because everything was very messy and cluttered.

When I reached up and took the yellow bottle off the shelf, a

collection of odd-looking twigs and dried flowers nearly fell on top of me, but at the last minute Fairy G. waved her wand, and they flew back to the places they'd come from.

"Tell Fairy Angora to use the dust carefully, Amy," Fairy G. said. "It's powerful stuff. And remind her it only lasts a day or two."

"Yes, Fairy G.," I said. "Thank you very much!"

The marble hallway was gleaming as I came out of Fairy G.'s room. The maids had left, but the floor was still a little bit wet. I walked very carefully, and I'd almost gotten back to our classroom when I sneezed—and my feet slid out from under me. I grabbed at the door to save myself, and dropped the yellow bottle—and it crashed to the floor and broke into a million little pieces.

Chapter Three

"Oh, no!" I wailed. "Oh, no."

I didn't know what to do. I stared at the mess in horror, my heart thumping in my chest—and then the strangest feeling crept into my head. It felt like fog in my brain. I couldn't remember where I

was or why I was looking at lots of
yellow powder and broken glass
spread in front of me.

The door beside me opened and
Fairy Angora popped her head out.

"Amy!" she said. "What was that crash? Are you all right?" And then she saw the mess. "Is that the Forgetting Dust? Quick! Come inside." She grabbed my hand and

pulled me into the classroom. As
she slammed the door behind me, a
little cloud of yellow powder flew
into the air and the foggy feeling in
my head grew stronger.

"Amy! Amy?" Fairy Angora

waved her wand over my head. "Do you know who I am?"

It was so weird! I knew that I knew her name—but I just couldn't think of what it was! "Um . . ." I began. "Um . . . I'm so sorry. . . ."

"Oooh! What's the matter with Amy?" asked a spiteful voice. "Has she lost her mind?"

I rubbed my head furiously. I knew who had spoken, but I couldn't remember her name either. Had I really lost my mind?

Fairy Angora tapped my shoulder twice with her wand and said, "Forgetting Dust, your task is done. Please leave Amy—three, two, *one*!"

My head cleared at once. "Thank you, Fairy Angora," I said. "I'm very sorry I dropped the bottle. Should I get a dustpan and broom?"

Fairy Angora shook her head. "Even though I've taken the spell away, you'd forget what you were doing after a second or two. Don't worry about it, my angel. Anyone can have an accident."

Then a spiteful voice, and I knew now that it belonged to Diamonde, said, "If you ask me, only clumsy people fall over and drop precious powders."

Gruella sniggered. "Clumsy people like elephant Amy."

"Diamonde! Gruella!" Fairy Angora was really annoyed. "I've had enough of your nasty little comments. Kindly go and sit in the corner until I say you can get up again." She watched the twins stomp across the room to the chairs in the corner, then she turned to the rest of us. "I'm very sorry, my dears, but I'll have to ask you to stay in this room until the Forgetting Dust is cleared away from outside. And don't go near the door either. I'll give you something to practice, and then I'll get Fairy G. to help me clean up the dust. Now, let's try those pirouettes again, shall we? Ready? One, two, three, *twirl*!"

And the most amazing thing happened. I found myself spinning

across the room as if I'd been doing
ballet all my life! It was so strange!
As I came to a stop on the other side
of the room, Fairy Angora clapped
her hands. "Well done, Amy," she

said. "That was wonderful. Five tiara points!"

There was a loud, angry snort from Diamonde. Gruella whispered, "That's not fair. You only got two points."

"I know. And I bet it's the magic dust that's making Amy do that," Diamonde hissed back.

Fairy Angora overheard her. "Actually, Diamonde, it isn't magic. Sometimes when you clear away Forgetting Dust, it makes your memory sharper. Did you do ballet when you were little, Amy?"

I nodded.

Fairy Angora beamed. "That

explains it, then. You're just remembering an old skill. Now, please get into groups. I'd like you to work out a dance sequence while I run and get Fairy G. After we've cleaned up the magic dust, I'll ask her to watch you dancing."

Of course all of us Poppy Roomers hurried together to make a group, and as usual Diamonde and Gruella decided they were going to work together. Fairy Angora waited until she saw we were busy, and then carefully

opened the door and slipped out.

As the door closed Diamonde hurried toward it and pulled Gruella behind her. "I want some of that magic powder," she said. "I just know that's what made stupid Amy dance like that—" She bent down, opened the door, and scooped as much Forgetting Dust as she could from the floor.

Chapter Four

*I*t was really weird!

Diamonde blinked, sneezed, and said in a squeaky voice, "Where am I?"

Gruella stared at her. "Don't be silly, Diamonde," she said. "You're at a ballet lesson!"

"Ballet?" Diamonde clapped her hands. "Ooooh! I love ballet!" And she hopped and thumped across the floor as if she were a toddler.

"Diamonde!" Gruella sounded

really scared. "Stop it!"

Princess Lauren shook her head. "I don't think she can stop," she said. "I think it's the Forgetting Dust working. She's forgotten how old she is."

"But she can't keep behaving like a two-year-old!" Gruella gasped. "We'll never get any extra tiara points if she can't dance properly."

"La da da dee, la da da dee!" Diamonde sang, and she did a little twirl and fell over. She sat on the floor and laughed. "Silly billy me! Diamonde did go all fall down!"

"I'm sure Fairy Angora will be able to take the spell off again,"

Georgia said hopefully. "She did with Amy."

"But she'll be really angry with Diamonde!" Gruella wailed. "She told us not to go near the door. And we have to get some more tiara points or we won't earn our Ruby Sashes tomorrow and get to go to Pearl Palace in the golden coach!"

I looked at Diamonde, who was sitting on the floor sucking her thumb. It was odd, but I couldn't help feeling just a little bit sorry for her and Gruella. I know the twins are horrible most of the time, but they do care about each other.

"Do you know what?" I said

slowly. "I might just have an idea."

"Do you really?" Gruella's eyes lit up. "Oh, Amy, if you help us, I

promise I'll be nice to you for ever and ever!"

"Well," I began, "it depends on whether the rest of the Poppy Room is willing to help."

"Of course we are!" Princess

Georgia sounded most indignant. "You know we will, Amy."

"That's right." Princess Jessica nodded hard. "The Poppy Room to the rescue!"

I smiled my thanks and went on, "Suppose we did a dance where we all pretended that Diamonde was pretending to be a little girl? And we were teaching her all the different ballet steps? That way we'd get to show off what we could do, and maybe Fairy Angora and Fairy G. won't notice she's under a spell until it wears off. Fairy G. told me it only lasts a day."

All my friends and Gruella

stared at me. "Amy!" Princess Chloe said. "That's so smart! How did you think of it? It's perfect!"

I could feel myself blushing. "Thanks very much," I mumbled. "Um, shall we get started?"

By the time Fairy Angora came back with Fairy G., we'd worked out a whole dance routine. I don't want to sound like I'm boasting, but it worked better than I'd even hoped. We showed Diamonde the different steps, and she laughed and clapped her hands, and did her best to copy us exactly as if she were two years old. It was actually a lot of fun—Diamonde was very sweet!

And Gruella was wonderful too, although we did keep having to tell her not to look so worried.

We knew when the two fairy godmothers were outside because

we heard Fairy G.'s voice booming,
"Forgetting Dust upon the ground,
back in the bottle, safe and sound!"

There was a bright yellow flash,
and then the door opened and

Fairy G. marched in with the bottle in her hand looking as if it had never been broken. Fairy Angora floated behind her, smiling happily. "There, my angels," she said. "All

better. And now show us what you've been doing."

We were the last to do our dance, and it was a little difficult while we were waiting because Diamonde kept whispering, "I want a cookie! I want some juice!" Luckily we managed to keep her quiet, although I did wonder if Fairy G. was peering in our direction once or twice.

When it was time to show off our routine, though, Diamonde was wonderful. Fairy G. and Fairy Angora clapped and clapped, and we were given fifteen tiara points each!

"Well done!" Fairy Angora was glowing, she was so pleased. "And I'm very happy that you've worked so hard, Diamonde. You've more than made up for your bad behavior earlier."

"Yes! Tank 'oo, nice fairy!" And before we could stop her, Diamonde rushed forward and gave Fairy Angora a huge hug. "I'm a good girl!" she said as she fluttered her eyelashes. "I'm pretty Princess Diamonde! Tee hee heee!" And she twirled around and around the room until she fell over again and sat laughing at us.

Chapter Five

"Diamonde!" Fairy Angora didn't look very pleased. "You don't need to keep pretending now, you know."

And Fairy G. didn't look very happy either. She folded her arms and looked stern. "I'm sorry to tell you, Fairy Angora, but Diamonde *isn't* pretending! If she's been near the magic dust, she won't remember anything that happened before she actually touched it. It seems to me there's been some very clever thinking here to cover up the use of the Forgetting Dust. Who is responsible for this?"

My heart began to thump in my chest, but I had to step forward. "Fairy G., it was me."

But all of a sudden the most amazing thing happened. Diamonde smiled and pulled herself to her feet, and said, "Amy is a good girl, big fairy! She showed Diamonde how to dance. It was me that played with the

fairy dust." She tilted her head to one side and rolled her eyes. "Diamonde is a bad girl." And she slapped her own wrist and giggled.

There was a long silence, and then Fairy G. began to laugh. She laughed and laughed, and before

long we were all laughing too—
even Gruella and Diamonde.

"You know," Fairy G. said as she
wiped her streaming eyes, "we don't
need a competition tomorrow. I
know exactly who should ride in
Queen Fabiola's golden coach and
lead the procession to Pearl Palace.
Princess Amy, you're a star! And so
are all of you girls from the Poppy
Room—and, I'm delighted to say,
Gruella as well. And I hope
Diamonde will appreciate just how
generous you've been, and how
very, very kind."

Fairy Angora nodded. "Should
we take the Forgetting Dust

away?" she asked.

Fairy G. stroked her chin thoughtfully. "I think perhaps we should," she said. "Forgetting Dust, your task is done. Leave Diamonde, three, two, one!"

Tiny yellow sparkles filled the air, and Diamonde rubbed her eyes and yawned as if she'd just woken up. She looked around at all of us and smiled a truly genuine smile.

"Hello," she said. "I've just had

the strangest dream. I dreamed I was little, and you were all being so kind to me. Thank you!"

Olivia nudged me. "Do you think she might have forgotten how to be mean?" she whispered.

"I don't know," I whispered back. "Let's just enjoy it while it lasts."

And we did. Diamonde went on being nice for the rest of the day, and the next day too. When we rode in the amazing golden coach to Pearl Palace, she insisted I sit in the very best seat. As we lined up in front of Queen Fabiola to receive our Ruby Sashes, she told

our principal that I was the nicest girl in the entire Princess Academy. As the music began for the End-of-Term Celebration Ball, she curtsied to me and said, "Amy, I know I've sometimes been mean to you, but can we be friends? Real friends?"

I smiled at her and said, "Of course we can!" And I really truly

meant it, but I couldn't help noticing that as the evening went on she tried harder and harder to be the best at every dance. When

she pushed Georgia out of the way
so she could take the biggest helping
of strawberry cake, I knew the spell
had finally worn off, but it had been
nice while it lasted.

And as I snuggled down in the Poppy Room that night, I thought, *I've got so many really wonderful friends that I don't mind if Diamonde and Gruella are sometimes mean.* There's Chloe and Olivia and Georgia and Lauren and Jessica—and best of all, there's *you*!

What happens next?

FIND OUT IN

Princess Hannah
~ AND THE ~
Little Black Kitten

Hello! I'm Princess Hannah, and I'm so glad you're here at Pearl Palace with me. Isabella, Lucy, Grace, Ellie, and Sarah are thrilled as well — have you met them yet? They're my friends in the Lily Room, and we do everything together. I'm really looking forward to this new year — although I hope the twins aren't too awful. You just never know what they'll think of next.

Visit all your favorite

The Tiara Club

Go to www.tiaraclubbooks.com

Tiara Club princesses!

The Tiara Club
AT SILVER TOWERS

for games, puzzles, and more fun!

You are cordially invited
to the Royal Princess Academy.

Introducing the new class of princesses
at Ruby Mansions

Katherine Tegen Books
An Imprint of HarperCollinsPublishers

HarperTrophy®
An Imprint of HarperCollinsPublishers